The Tiara Club

at Emerald Castle

Princess Ruby

and the Enchanted Whale

By Vivian French

ORCHARD BOOKS

The Royal Palace Academy
for the Preparation of Perfect Princesses

(Known to our students as "*The Princess Academy*")

OUR SCHOOL MOTTO:
*A Perfect Princess always thinks of others
before herself, and is kind, caring and truthful.*

Emerald Castle offers a complete education for
Tiara Club princesses while taking full advantage of
our seaside situation. The curriculum includes:

A visit to Emerald Sea World Aquarium and Education Pool	*Swimming lessons (safely supervised at all times)*
A visit to Seabird Island	*Whale watching*

Our headteacher, Queen Gwendoline, is present at all
times, and students are well looked after by the school
Fairy Godmother, Fairy Angora.

Our resident staff and visiting experts include:

QUEEN MOLLY (Sports and games)	*KING JONATHAN (Captain of the Royal Yacht)*
LORD HENRY (Natural History)	*QUEEN MOTHER MATILDA (Etiquette, Posture and Flower Arranging)*

We award tiara points to encourage our Tiara Club princesses towards the next level. All princesses who win enough points at Emerald Castle will be presented with their Emerald Sashes and attend a celebration ball.

Emerald Sash Tiara Club princesses are invited to return to Diamond Turrets, our superb residence for Perfect Princesses, where they may continue their education at a higher level.

PLEASE NOTE:
Princesses are expected to arrive at the Academy with a *minimum* of:

Twenty ballgowns
(with all necessary hoops, petticoats, etc)

Twelve day dresses

Seven gowns
suitable for garden parties, and other special day occasions

Twelve tiaras

Dancing shoes
five pairs

Velvet slippers
three pairs

Riding boots
two pairs

Swimming costumes, playsuits, parasols, sun hats and other essential outdoor accessories as required

Are you good at singing? I'm not.
If I'm honest, even frogs hop away and
hide under their lily pads when I sing.
But Perfect Princesses are supposed to
be able to sing like nightingales – at least,
that's what Queen Mother Matilda says.
Ooops – I'm so sorry! I haven't introduced
myself. I'm Princess Ruby. Have you met
the other princesses from Daffodil Room?
Amelia, Leah, Millie, Rachel and Zoe?
They're like me. VERY pleased
you're here with us!

Chapter One

"La la la LAH! La la la LAH! La la la la la la LAH!"

I could see Queen Mother Matilda was turning purple, but what could I do?

"Princess Ruby!" she snapped. "You are NOT trying! Take three minus tiara points, and make sure you do better next lesson!"

Then she gathered up her music sheets and swept away from the piano and out of the music room. I sighed, and Millie patted my shoulder.

"Never mind, Ruby," she said. "I think you've got a lovely voice. It's just...different."

Diamonde was standing beside me, and she nudged her twin sister. "Perfect Princesses ALWAYS sing in tune, don't they, Gruella?"

"That's what Mummy says," Gruella agreed.

"So anyone who doesn't sing in tune can't EVER be a Perfect Princess!" Diamonde said smugly, and she gave me SUCH a superior look.

Amelia made a face as the twins skipped out of the music room hand in hand. "Why do they always have to be so horrid?" she asked.

Zoe looked wise. "I think it's

their mother's fault," she said. "My dad met her once, and she never stopped talking about the twins and how totally perfect they were. He said he actually felt sorry for them, because he could tell they were completely spoiled."

"That's right," Leah nodded. "And because there are two of them they can stick together, and they don't mind what anyone else thinks."

Rachel sighed. "It's still very annoying, though."

"Just take no notice of them," said Millie. Then she grinned SUCH a wicked grin. "'A Perfect Princess will ALWAYS ignore beetles, spiders and annoying twins!'"

That made us all giggle, because Millie sounded SO like our headteacher, Queen Gwendoline, and I began to feel a bit better – but I still had tomorrow to worry about.

"How can I get better at singing?" I asked Rachel as we walked along the corridor to the recreation room. "I don't want any more minus tiara points. I've got far too many already – I'm really scared I won't win my Emerald Sash at the end of term."

Rachel rubbed her nose thoughtfully, and then, as we passed an open door, she grabbed my arm. "Look! Fairy G's in her room, and the door's open – go and ask her. If anyone can help, she will. After all, she IS the school fairy godmother!"

She looked up, and there were tears in her eyes. "No, Ruby my dear, I'm not." She heaved a huge sigh, and waved me towards a chair.

"That's a really good idea," I said, and I tapped politely on the door before going in.

Fairy G is one of my most favourite teachers; she's almost always cheerful, and she has the biggest booming voice you've ever heard. And she wears the most un-fairylike boots, and stomps about Emerald Castle making sure that everything's in order – but when I went into her room she was sitting at her desk with her head in her hands.

"Fairy G!" I said in surprise. "Are you all right?"

"Every year something very wonderful happens here at Emerald Castle, something very special. A group of grey whales swim past on their way to the feeding grounds in the northern seas, and Old Grey – the oldest of them all – sings to us as she passes by. My great-grandmother made friends with her a long, long time ago, and she's sung every year since then. She brings a very special magic to Emerald Castle and all our students... But although we know the whales have come this year, because the fishermen have seen them, Old Grey isn't with them."

"Oh – I'm so sorry," I said, and I was. I felt really sorry for Fairy G, and I tried to think of something helpful to say. "Could she have got held up somehow, and be behind the others, do you think?"

Fairy G shook her head. "She's always one of the first...but I suppose she could be getting slow. She must be very old now..."

And then our fairy godmother suddenly sat up straight, and her eyes began to shine. "Thank you, Ruby. You could be right; she might have been held up. And I've made a decision! I'm going to ask Queen Gwendoline if we can borrow the royal yacht and see for ourselves! We'll go tomorrow, and look for Old Grey!"

Chapter Two

We were all SO excited when we heard that Queen Gwendoline had said we could go out on her yacht to look for the whales. Even the twins looked thrilled.

"The royal yacht has the most TERRIBLY handsome sailors," Diamonde said, her eyes sparkling. "And Mummy says they're ALL

21

princes, doesn't she, Gruella?"

Gruella nodded. "They drive the yacht as well, Mummy says."

"Silly!" Diamonde began to snigger. "The princes don't DRIVE boats, Gruella. They STEER them. EVERYBODY knows that."

Gruella looked cross. "Well, I didn't, so there."

Diamonde stopped sniggering, and looked thoughtful. "Of course, we'll have to wear our VERY best dresses. What are you going to wear, Ruby?"

"Me?" I was surprised she'd asked me. "Erm...I'm not sure."

"Fairy G wants us to wear our sailor uniforms," Zoe chipped in. "I saw her pinning a notice on the board, and I stopped to read it. It said, 'All princesses will be expected to wear sailor dresses and sensible shoes.'"

I saw Diamonde and Gruella

look at each other, and it was SO obvious they thought that was the worst idea ever. All they said, though, was "Really?" and then they hurried away.

Millie smiled. "I wonder what they'll wear?"

"We'll find out tomorrow," Leah said. "I bet it's something totally ridiculous."

Leah was right. When we came down to breakfast the next day, the twins were wearing sailor dresses, but they were SO different from ours! They were made of satin with really long skirts, and looked like ballgowns. Diamonde looked at our uniforms, and turned up her nose.

"You DO look plain," she said. "Don't you think you should make some sort of an effort? What will the princes think?"

"They'll think our princesses are extremely sensible," Fairy G announced, as she stamped up to where we were sitting. "Diamonde and Gruella, please go upstairs and change."

Diamonde stuck out her lower lip. "But THESE are our sailor dresses, Fairy G. We haven't got anything else."

Fairy G put her hands on her hips. "Very well, Diamonde. You and Gruella may wear those ridiculous outfits, but don't blame me if they get spoiled. Now, I want everyone outside in exactly ten minutes, and we'll walk down to the landing stage."

Diamonde's mouth opened, and I just knew she was going to say, "Perfect Princesses NEVER walk," but then she saw Fairy G's expression, and changed her mind.

Instead she made a big fuss of arranging her skirts as she got up from the table.

"Come along, Gruella," she said in her bossiest voice. "At least TWO of us will look like Perfect Princesses when we reach the royal yacht!"

Chapter Three

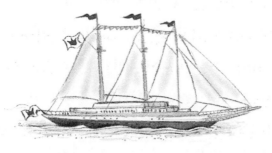

The royal yacht was just WONDERFUL. It was painted a fabulous royal blue on the outside, but inside everything was either a lovely golden wood, or crisp white, like the sails. As we walked up the gangway behind Fairy G, the captain came forward to greet us, and a row of smart-looking sailors saluted. A very small sailor handed us each a life jacket as we stepped on board, and we thanked him politely – all except for the twins.

"I can't wear this!" Diamonde stepped backwards in horror. "It's HIDEOUS!"

"It'll RUIN our dresses!"
Gruella agreed.

Fairy G frowned. "If you don't
wear life jackets, you can't come
on board."

The twins looked at each other,
and then, very unwillingly, did as
they were told.

"That's better," Fairy G said, and turned to the captain. "Good morning, King Jonathan! May I present the princesses from Emerald Castle? I'm sure Queen Gwendoline has told you why we're here."

Princess Ruby's
stickers

The **Tiara** Club

Ruby

*Discover more magical stickers
in the other Emerald Castle books!*

www.tiaraclub.co.uk

Tiara Club series is written by Vivian French.   www.orchardbooks.co.uk

ORCHARD BOOKS

King Jonathan nodded. "We spotted a group of whales only yesterday," he said, "but I understand you're looking for one whale in particular?"

"That's right," Fairy G gave a tiny sigh. "Old Grey..."

The king's face lit up. "Old Grey? But she's been coming this way for years. She always sings as she passes Emerald Castle, and it's really beautiful."

"But she hasn't been heard this year," Fairy G told him, "and I'm worried about her."

"We'll find her," King Jonathan said firmly. "I'll send a couple of lads up to the crow's nest, and they can keep a look out." He blew sharply on a silver whistle, and two sailors came running towards us.

"Prince Fritz and Prince Malcolm – collect a couple of telescopes, and take your positions in the crow's nest. You're looking out for either a group of grey whales, or a whale on her own; shout down as soon as you see anything."

"Aye aye, Captain!" The princes saluted the king, and dashed away. A few moments later we saw them positively zooming up

a rope ladder, and the next minute
they were in the crow's nest at the
very top of the mast.

"Right!" King Jonathan blew on his whistle again, and at once all the sailor princes leapt into action. They hauled up the anchor and heaved in the mooring ropes, and as Fairy G shepherded us out of the way we could see the heavy main sail beginning to fill and billow out like a huge white cloud. A moment later we were moving, faster and faster.

"Doesn't it feel wonderful?" Millie said, as the yacht leant into the wind and fairly flew over the waves.

"It's utterly gorgeous!" Amelia's cheeks were very pink. "I've never been on a sailing boat before."

Fairy G smiled. "All we need now is to find the whales, and it'll be a perfect day out."

"Won't they be scared of us?" Rachel asked.

One of the sailors heard her, and he stopped beside us. "A sailing ship is the best way to see whales," he explained. "Motor boats leave pollution in the water, and the sound of the engine can disturb the whales' sense of direction."

"Thank you," Rachel said shyly, but Diamonde elbowed her out of the way.

"I feel sick," she announced, but before anyone could answer there was a loud shout from above. The little sailor who'd given us our life jackets came running towards us.

"If you please, your majesties," he gasped, "the whales are on the starboard bow!"

As he turned and dashed away again Fairy G jumped to her feet. "Goodness! I never thought we'd find them so soon! Come along – come and see your first ever grey whales!" She hurried to the right hand side of the boat, and leant over the rail.

"Quickly!" she called. "Come and see!"

Chapter Four

Have you ever seen a real live grey whale? I never had – and I had NO idea just how absolutely VAST they are. Vast, and somehow terribly dignified and special. Even though we weren't far away they took no notice of us, but moved steadily on and on through the blue-green water.

I stared and stared and STARED, and I couldn't say a word.

"Is Old Grey with them?" Zoe asked Fairy G. "Will she sing for us now?"

Fairy G was squinting into the sunshine. "I can't see her," she said. "It's easy to spot her; she's got a crown of barnacles on her

head...she looks almost as if she's wearing a tiara."

King Jonathan came striding across the deck to join us.

"Splendid, aren't they?" He smiled as he watched one of the whales dive deep into the sea and then rise up again to blow a spout of water high up into the air.

The water drops glittered and shone, and I couldn't help taking a deep breath – it was SO beautiful.

"Could we sail back the way they've come?" Fairy G asked hopefully. "Just in case Old Grey is following on behind them?"

"I have a different idea." King Jonathan blew on his whistle, and there was another flurry of activity.

We watched in amazement as the sails were lowered and tidied away, and the anchor was rattled overboard with a massive *Splash*!

It all happened so fast that it seemed no time at all before the royal yacht was rocking peacefully on the waves.

"If we wait here," King Jonathan told us, "we can all watch for Old Grey. She'll follow the same sea path as the rest of her family, so we're unlikely to miss her. And while we're waiting, perhaps the princesses would like to take turns keeping a look out?"

I looked up at the crow's nest on the top of the mast, and my stomach did fifty somersaults. I am SO not good at heights! But the king saw me going pale, and he laughed.

"I wasn't suggesting you climbed up there, my dear," he said. "There's an excellent lookout position on the bows." And he pointed to the front of the yacht.

"Oh," I said, and I blushed. "Yes – I'd love to help look."

Diamonde grabbed Gruella, and they both made the king a deep curtsey. "Perhaps my sister and I could help Ruby?" she asked.

"Mummy says we have SUCH sharp eyes!"

I'd been hoping Amelia, Leah and the rest of Daffodil Room would be able to come with me, but King Jonathan nodded at the twins. "Of course you can," he said, and he turned to a tall sailor who was standing nearby.

"Prince Lazlo, would you escort these princesses to the bows? And make sure they're comfortable."

Diamonde gave Prince Lazlo what she obviously thought was a dazzling smile, and I suddenly realised why she'd wanted to come with me. There were sailor princes sitting and standing all along the deck, and she and Gruella paraded all the way to the bows, simpering and curtseying and swishing their long dresses as they went. One or two of the sailors stood to attention and bowed back, but most of them just looked surprised.

"Thank you, thank you all!" Diamonde called, and flung herself into one of the chairs that the littlest sailor had rushed to put in place. At exactly the same time Gruella gave her most gracious smile and a wave, and sank into the chair from the other side...

And there were the two of them squashed in together.

Chapter Five

Diamonde stopped simpering, and looked FURIOUS.

"Get off me!" she hissed at Gruella – but Gruella couldn't move.

"YOU get off!" she snapped, but Diamonde was just as stuck. I caught the eye of the littlest sailor, and I knew he was trying his very best not to laugh – his face was scarlet. The other sailors weren't so polite, however; a few turned away, but most of them absolutely roared until tears rolled down their cheeks.

And do you know what? I actually felt sorry for Diamonde and Gruella. They looked SO silly, and there was nothing they could do about it.

I stepped forward, and took Diamonde's hands, and pulled... and pulled...

And the littlest sailor jumped forward and held the back of the chair, and suddenly...

THUMP!

Diamonde landed on the deck in the most undignified flurry of skirts and petticoats, leaving a pink and flustered Gruella in the chair. Diamonde tried to get to her feet, but she kept stepping on her long dress, and I had to help

her up. Her face was even redder than the littlest sailor's, and I knew she was trying not to cry – and then she absolutely glared at me.

"It's all YOUR fault!" she shouted, and she gave me a massive push.

I stepped back, staggered, and slipped...and as Diamonde and Gruella screamed, I slid across the deck. If I hadn't grabbed at the rail I would have fallen overboard; as it was I ended up staring down into the water...

And an eye stared back at me.

"What?" I gasped.

And then I realised – it was a whale. Not a vast, enormous one, but a baby whale...not much longer than four or five metres. I carefully stood up, and there was Fairy G right behind me.

"Did you see?" I whispered, and she nodded.

"So THAT'S why Old Grey was late this year." Fairy G sounded so happy I couldn't help smiling too. "And look – there she is!"

We all turned, and Fairy G was right. Not far away was the most extraordinarily large whale, and as we gazed at her she blew a spout of water way, way up into the air. Then she dived, and the waves creamed and curled about her.

A moment later she appeared again, and this time the little one was next to her, close to her side. Two spouts soared into the air, and a rainbow of sparkling water drops surrounded Old Grey and her baby.

And then Old Grey began to sing.

What did it sound like?

I really, really can't describe it...except to say it was beautiful. It wasn't like human singing; it was more as if a mountain or the sea itself were singing. It made tingles go up and down my spine, and I wanted to laugh and cry all at the same time. Every single person on the royal yacht stood completely still, hardly breathing, until gradually the song faded away...and we realised that Old Grey and her baby had gone.

"WOW!" Zoe said. "That's

made me feel...I don't know. All peaceful and lovely inside."

"Me too," Millie agreed, and Leah nodded, a dreamy look on her face.

Amelia sighed happily. "It was...I can't think of the word..."

"Magical," Rachel said, and we all nodded.

A second later something else magical happened. Diamonde and Gruella walked up to me, looking very shamefaced. Gruella said, "Sorry, Ruby. Thank you for helping us." And then Diamonde shuffled her feet, and gave me a sideways look.

"I was really mean," she said. "I'm sorry, Ruby. I really truly am."

Chapter Six

I don't know what Fairy G would have done if the twins hadn't apologised, but as it was she looked amazingly cheerful.

"Time to go back to Emerald Castle!" she announced.

King Jonathan picked up his silver whistle, and then paused. "I think we've all been very honoured," he said, "and I think we should celebrate. Fairy G, have you got your wand with you?"

Fairy G smiled. "Of course."

"In that case," King Jonathan said, "we should have a party... a celebration. I happen to know that some of my lads can play a very jolly tune, and the cooks have already prepared a splendid meal...so what do you think?"

In answer Fairy G waved her wand...and immediately the royal yacht was hung with bunches of blue and silver ribbon, while tiny silver bells tinkled from every rope. Blue and silver cushions were scattered over the deck, and as the cooks arrived carrying plates and plates of the most delicious food, tables sprang up from nowhere.

"We'll eat first, and dance afterwards," King Jonathan declared.

And that's what we did – all except for Diamonde and Gruella.

They went down to the cabin, and said they didn't want to dance.

"Shall I go and see if they're all right?" I asked Fairy G, but she shook her head.

"It won't hurt them to have a little think about the way they behave," she said, but she didn't sound cross, just thoughtful.

Zoe touched Fairy G's arm. "Was it the whale song that made them change?"

"I think it might have been." Fairy G smiled down at us. "Enchantment is a very strange thing. Now, off you go! I can hear someone beginning to play a conga!"

After the dancing – which was SUCH fun! – we sat down on the cushions, and Prince Fritz played the accordion as we sang sea shanties...

And King Jonathan actually said he liked my singing!

*

When we were finally back at Emerald Castle, and trailing up the stairs to Daffodil Room, I found myself humming one of the songs.

"Do you know what?" Amelia said. "I think you're much more in tune now, Ruby."

Leah giggled. "Maybe it was hearing Old Grey!"

I thought they were just being kind, because they were my friends.

But guess what happened! The next day we had another singing lesson, and Queen Mother Matilda said I was MUCH improved!

I think the effect of the enchanted whale song must have worn off, because Diamonde and Gruella snorted rudely...

But I didn't mind.

I've got lots of other wonderful friends...and YOU'RE one of the best!

Don't miss  *website at:*

www.tiaraclub.co.uk

Keep up to date with the latest
Tiara Club books and meet all
your favourite princesses!

There is SO much to see and do,
including games and activities. You can
even become an exclusive member of the
Tiara Club Princess Academy.

PLUS, there's an exciting
Emerald Castle competition
with a truly AMAZING prize!

Be a Perfect Princess — check it out today!

What happens next?
Find out in
Princess Millie
and the Magical Mermaid

Good day, pretty princess! Greetings
from thy faithful friend, Princess Millie!
Eeeek – wouldn't it be SUCH hard work if we
had to talk like that all the time? It's much
nicer to be able to say, "Hi! How are you?"
Isn't it so lovely here at Emerald Castle?
Amelia, Leah, Ruby, Rachel, Zoe and I just
ADORE being by the sea. We lie in bed in
Daffodil Room and listen to the waves...and
wonder what the horrible twins will do next!

I think art lessons are my most favourite, especially when we get to go outside. I always go into a sort of dream, and when Queen Molly took us to a rocky beach to paint a sea scene for our school art competition I was SO happy. There were heaps of seaweedy rocks scattered everywhere, just as if a giant had flung handfuls of huge boulders onto the sandy shore, and I was just wondering if I'd drawn them properly when—

"Princess Millie! What a LOVELY picture!"

Queen Molly was standing RIGHT behind me, and I nearly

jumped out of my skin. My paint box went flying one way, and my water jar went the other – ALL over Diamonde. She let out a massive screech, and leapt to her feet.

"You did that on purpose, Millie!" Her eyes were positively flashing as she glared at me. "I know you did!"

"I'm really sorry," I apologised, and I searched in my bag for a clean hankie. "Here – use this."

Diamonde ignored me, and turned to Queen Molly. "Can I go back to Emerald Castle? Millie's absolutely RUINED my dress! Mummy'll be FURIOUS – it's the very best satin, you know."

"Rubbish, Diamonde." Queen Molly gave one of her loud cheery laughs. "It's only a drop of water. If you sit over there in the sunshine you'll dry out in no time at all."

Diamonde stuck out her lower lip, but she didn't argue. She picked up her drawing book and paints and stomped off towards an especially large rock, and after a moment or two Gruella went after her.

~ *Want to read more?* ~
Princess Mille and the Magical Mermaid is out now!

This summer, look out for

Emerald Ball

ISBN: 978 1 84616 881 9

Two stories in one fabulous book!